C000180543

'"Watch ou[t] the mosc[...] they called to one another, lyrically because warning wasn't any use any- way, as they walked out of their kimonos and dropped them like the petals of one big scattered flower on the bank behind them, and exposing themselves felt in a hundred places at once the little pangs'

EUDORA WELTY
Born 13 April 1909, Jackson, Mississippi
Died 23 July 2001, Jackson, Mississippi

'Moon Lake' was first published in book form in *The Golden Apples*, Boston, 1949.

EUDORA WELTY

Moon Lake

PENGUIN BOOKS

PENGUIN CLASSICS

Published by the Penguin Group
Penguin Books Ltd, 80 Strand, London WC2R ORL, England
Penguin Group (USA) Inc., 375 Hudson Street, New York, New York 10014, USA
Penguin Group (Canada), 90 Eglinton Avenue East, Suite 700, Toronto, Ontario,
Canada M4P 2Y3 (a division of Pearson Penguin Canada Inc.)
Penguin Ireland, 25 St Stephen's Green, Dublin 2, Ireland (a division of Penguin Books Ltd)
Penguin Group (Australia), 250 Camberwell Road, Camberwell, Victoria 3124, Australia
(a division of Pearson Australia Group Pty Ltd)
Penguin Books India Pvt Ltd, 11 Community Centre, Panchsheel Park,
New Delhi – 110 017, India
Penguin Group (NZ), 67 Apollo Drive, Rosedale, North Shore 0632, New Zealand
(a division of Pearson New Zealand Ltd)
Penguin Books (South Africa) (Pty) Ltd, 24 Sturdee Avenue, Rosebank, Johannesburg 2196,
South Africa

Penguin Books Ltd, Registered Offices: 80 Strand, London WC2R ORL, England

www.penguin.com

Selected from *The Collected Stories of Eudora Welty*, first published in Great Britain by
Marion Boyars Publishers Ltd 1981
This edition published in Penguin Classics 2011

3

Copyright © Eudora Welty, 1980

All rights reserved

Typeset by Jouve (UK), Milton Keynes
Printed in England by Clays Ltd, St Ives plc

Except in the United States of America, this book is sold subject
to the condition that it shall not, by way of trade or otherwise, be lent,
re-sold, hired out, or otherwise circulated without the publisher's
prior consent in any form of binding or cover other than that in
which it is published and without a similar condition including this
condition being imposed on the subsequent purchaser

ISBN: 978-0-141-19627-5

www.greenpenguin.co.uk

Mixed Sources
Product group from well-managed
forests and other controlled sources
www.fsc.org Cert no. SA-COC-1592
© 1996 Forest Stewardship Council

Penguin Books is committed to a sustainable future
for our business, our readers and our planet.
The book in your hands is made from paper
certified by the Forest Stewardship Council.

Moon Lake

I

From the beginning his martyred presence seriously affected them. They had a disquieting familiarity with it, hearing the spit of his despising that went into his bugle. At times they could hardly recognize what he thought he was playing. Loch Morrison, Boy Scout and Life Saver, was under the ordeal of a week's camp on Moon Lake with girls.

Half the girls were county orphans, wished on them by Mr Nesbitt and the Men's Bible Class after Billy Sunday's visit to town; but all girls, orphans and Morgana girls alike, were the same thing to Loch; maybe he threw in the two councilors too. He was hating every day of the seven. He hardly spoke; he never spoke first. Sometimes he swung in the trees; Nina Carmichael in particular would hear him crashing in the foliage somewhere when she was lying rigid in siesta.

While they were in the lake, for the dip or the five-o'clock swimming period in the afternoon, he stood against a tree with his arms folded, jacked up one-legged, sitting on his heel, as absolutely tolerant as an old fellow waiting for the store to open, being held up by the wall. Waiting for the girls to get out, he gazed upon some undisturbed part of the water. He despised their predicaments, most of all their not being able to swim. Sometimes he would take aim and from his right cheek shoot an imaginary gun at something far out, where they never were. Then he resumed his pose. He had been roped into this by his mother.

At the hours too hot for girls he used Moon Lake. He dived high off the crosspiece nailed up in the big oak, where the American Legion dived. He went through the air rocking and jerking like an engine, splashed in, climbed out, spat, climbed up again, dived off. He wore a long bathing suit which stretched longer from Monday to Tuesday and from Tuesday to Wednesday and so on, yawning at the armholes toward infinity, and it looked black and formal as a minstrel suit as he stood skinny against the clouds as on a stage.

He came and got his food and turned his back and ate it all alone like a dog and lived in a tent by himself, apart like the cook, and dived alone when the lake was clear of girls. That way, he seemed able to bear it; that would be his life. In early evening, in moonlight sings, the Boy Scout and Life Saver kept far away. They would sing 'When all the little ships come sailing home,' and he would be roaming off; they could tell about where he was. He played taps for them, invisibly then, and so beautifully they wept together, whole tentfuls some nights. Off with the whip-poor-wills and the coons and the owls and the little bobwhites – down where it all sloped away, he had pitched his tent, and slept there. Then at reveille, how he would spit into that cornet.

Reveille was his. He harangued the woods when the little minnows were trembling and running wizardlike in the water's edge. And how lovely and altered the trees were then, weighted with dew, leaning on one another's shoulders and smelling like big wet flowers. He blew his horn into their presence – trees' and girls' – and then watched the Dip.

'Good morning, Mr Dip, Dip, Dip, with your water just as cold as ice!' sang Mrs Gruenwald hoarsely. She took them for the dip, for Miss Moody said she couldn't, simply couldn't.

The orphans usually hung to the rear, and every other moment stood swayback with knees locked, the shoulders of their wash dresses ironed flat and stuck in peaks, and stared. For swimming they owned no bathing suits and went in in their underbodies. Even in the water they would stand swayback, each with a fist in front of her over the rope, looking over the flat surface as over the top of a tall mountain none of them could ever get over. Even at this hour of the day, they seemed to be expecting little tasks, something more immediate – little tasks that were never given out.

Mrs Gruenwald was from the North and said 'dup.' 'Good morning, Mr Dup, Dup, Dup, with your water just as cold as ice!' sang Mrs Gruenwald, fatly capering and leading them all in a singing, petering-out string down to the lake. She did a sort of little rocking dance in her exhortation, broad in her bathrobe. From the tail end of the line she looked like a Shredded Wheat Biscuit box rocking on its corners.

Nina Carmichael thought, There is nobody and nothing named Mr Dip, it is not a good morning until you have had coffee, and the water is the temperature of a just-cooling biscuit, thank Goodness. I hate this little parade of us girls, Nina thought, trotting fiercely in the center of it. It ruins the woods, all right. 'Gee, we think you're mighty nice,' they sang to Mr Dip, while the Boy Scout, waiting at the lake, watched them go in.

'Watch out for mosquitoes,' they called to one another, lyrically because warning wasn't any use anyway, as they walked out of their kimonos and dropped them like the petals of one big scattered flower on the bank behind them, and exposing themselves felt in a hundred places at once the little pangs. The orphans ripped their dresses off over their heads and stood in their underbodies. Busily they hung and piled their dresses on a cedar branch, obeying one of their own number, like a whole flock of ferocious little birds with pale topknots building themselves a nest. The orphan named Easter appeared in charge. She handed her dress wrong-side-out to a friend, who turned it and hung it up for her, and waited standing very still, her little fingers locked.

'Let's let the orphans go in the water first and get the snakes stirred up, Mrs Gruenwald,' Jinny Love Stark suggested first off, in the cheerful voice she adopted toward grown people. 'Then they'll be chased away by the time *we* go in.'

That made the orphans scatter in their pantie-waists, outwards from Easter; the little gauzes of gnats they ran through made them beat their hands at the air. They ran back together again, to Easter, and stood excitedly, almost hopping.

'I think we'll all go in in one big bunch,' Mrs Gruenwald said. Jinny Love lamented and beat against Mrs Gruenwald, Mrs Gruenwald's solid, rope-draped stomach all but returning her blows. 'All take hands – march! Into the water! *Don't* let the stobs and cypress roots break your legs! *Do* your best! Kick! Stay on top if you can and hold the rope if necessary!'

Mrs Gruenwald abruptly walked away from Jinny Love, out of the bathrobe, and entered the lake with a vast displacing. She left them on the bank with her Yankee advice.

The Morgana girls might never have gone in if the orphans hadn't balked. Easter came to a dead stop at Moon Lake and looked at it squinting as though it floated really on the Moon. And mightn't it be on the Moon? – it was a strange place, Nina thought, unlikely – and three miles from Morgana, Mississippi, all the time. The Morgana girls pulled the orphans' hands and dragged them in, or pushed suddenly from behind, and finally the orphans took hold of one another and waded forward in a body, singing 'Good Morning' with their stiff, chiplike lips. None of them could or would swim, ever, and they just stood waist-deep and waited for the dip to be over. A few of them reached out and caught the struggling Morgana girls by the legs as they splashed from one barky post to another, to see how hard it really was to stay up.

'Mrs Gruenwald, look, they want to drown us.'

But Mrs Gruenwald all this time was rising and sinking like a whale, she was in a sea of her own waves and perhaps of self-generated cold, out in the middle of the lake. She cared little that Morgana girls who learned to swim were getting a dollar from home. She had deserted them, no, she had never really been with them. Not only orphans had she deserted. In the water she kept so much to the profile that her single pushing-out eyeball looked like a little bottle of something. It was said she believed in evolution.

While the Boy Scout in the rosy light under the green trees twirled his horn so that it glittered and ran a puzzle in the sun, and emptied the spit out of it, he yawned, snappingly – as if he would bite the day, as quickly as Easter had bitten Deacon Nesbitt's hand on Opening Day.

'Gee, we think you're mighty nice,' they sang to Mr Dip, gasping, pounding their legs in him. If they let their feet go down, the invisible bottom of the lake felt like soft, knee-deep fur. The sharp hard knobs came up where least expected. The Morgana girls of course wore bathing slippers, and the mud loved to suck them off. The alligators had been beaten out of this lake, but it was said that water snakes – pilots – were swimming here and there; they would bite you but not kill you; and one cottonmouth moccasin was still getting away from the Negroes – if the Negroes were still going after him; he would kill you. These were the chances of getting sucked under, of being bitten, and of dying three miles away from home.

The brown water cutting her off at the chest, Easter looked directly before her, wide awake, unsmiling. Before she could hold a stare like that, she would have had to swallow something big – so Nina felt. It would have been something so big that it didn't matter to her what the inside of a snake's mouth was lined with. At the other end of her gaze the life saver grew almost insignificant. Her gaze moved like a little switch or wand, and the life saver scratched himself with his bugle, raked himself, as if that eased him. Yet the flick of a blue-bottle fly made Easter jump.

They swam and held to the rope, hungry and waiting. But they had to keep waiting till Loch Morrison blew his horn before they could come out of Moon Lake. Mrs Gruenwald, who capered before breakfast, believed in evolution, and put her face in the water, was quarter of a mile out. If she said anything, they couldn't hear her for the frogs.

II

Nina and Jinny Love, with the soles of their feet shocked from the walk, found Easter ahead of them down at the spring.

For the orphans, from the first, sniffed out the way to

the spring by themselves, and they could get there without stops to hold up their feet and pull out thorns and stickers, and could run through the sandy bottoms and never look down where they were going, and could grab hold with their toes on the sharp rutted path up the pine ridge and down. They clearly could never get enough of skimming over the silk-slick needles and setting prints of their feet in the bed of the spring to see them dissolve away under their eyes. What was it to them if the spring was muddied by the time Jinny Love Stark got there?

The one named Easter could fall flat as a boy, elbows cocked, and drink from the cup of her hand with her face in the spring. Jinny Love prodded Nina, and while they looked on Easter's drawers, Nina was opening the drinking cup she had brought with her, then collapsing it, feeling like a lady with a fan. That way, she was going over a thought, a fact: Half the people out here with me are orphans. Orphans. Orphans. She yearned for her heart to twist. But it didn't, not in time. Easter was through drinking – wiping her mouth and flinging her hand as if to break the bones, to get rid of the drops, and it was Nina's turn with her drinking cup.

Nina stood and bent over from the waist. Calmly, she held her cup in the spring and watched it fill. They could all see how it spangled like a cold star in the curling water. The water tasted the silver cool of the rim it went over running to her lips, and at moments the cup gave her teeth a pang. Nina heard her own throat swallowing. She paused and threw a smile about her. After she had drunk she wiped the cup on her tie and collapsed it, and put the little top on, and its ring over her finger. With that, Easter, one arm tilted, charged against the green bank and mounted it. Nina felt her surveying the spring and all from above. Jinny Love was down drinking like a chicken, kissing the water only.

Easter was dominant among the orphans. It was not that she was so bad. The one called Geneva stole, for example, but Easter was dominant for what she was in herself – for the way she held still, sometimes. All orphans were at once wondering and stoic – at one moment loving everything too much, the next folding back from it, tightly as hard green buds growing in the wrong direction, closing as they go. But it was as if Easter signaled them. Now she just stood up there, watching the spring, with the name Easter – tacky name, as Jinny Love Stark was the first to say. She was medium size, but her hair seemed to fly up at the temples, being cropped and wiry, and this crest made her nearly as tall as Jinny Love Stark. The rest of the orphans had hair paler than their tanned foreheads – straight and tow, the greenish yellow of cornsilk that dimmed black at the roots and shadows, with burnt-out-looking

bangs like young boys' and old men's hair; that was
from picking in the fields. Easter's hair was a withstand-
ing gold. Around the back of her neck beneath the hair
was a dark band on her skin like the mark a gold brace-
let leaves on the arm. It came to the Morgana girls with
a feeling of elation: the ring was pure dirt. They liked to
look at it, or to remember, too late, what it was – as
now, when Easter had already lain down for a drink and
left the spring. They liked to walk behind her and see
her back, which seemed spectacular from crested gold
head to hard, tough heel. Mr Nesbitt, from the Bible
Class, took Easter by the wrist and turned her around
to him and looked just as hard at her front. She had
started her breasts. What Easter did was to bite his right
hand, his collection hand. It was wonderful to have with
them someone dangerous but not, so far, or provenly,
bad. When Nina's little lead-mold umbrella, the size of
a clover, a Crackerjack prize, was stolen the first night
of camp, that was Geneva, Easter's friend.

Jinny Love, after wiping her face with a hand-made
handkerchief, pulled out a deck of cards she had secretly
brought in her middy pocket. She dropped them down,
bright blue, on a sandy place by the spring. 'Let's play
cassino. Do they call you *Easter*?'

Down Easter jumped, from the height of the bank.
She came back to them. 'Cassino, what's that?'

'All right, what do *you* want to play?'

'All right, I'll play you mumblety-peg.'

'I don't know how you play that!' cried Nina.

'Who would ever want to know?' asked Jinny Love, closing the circle.

Easter flipped out a jack-knife and with her sawed fingernail shot out three blades.

'Do you carry that in the orphan asylum?' Jinny Love asked with some respect.

Easter dropped to her scarred and coral-colored knees. They saw the dirt. 'Get down if you want to play me mumblety-peg,' was all she said, 'and watch out for your hands and faces.'

They huddled down on the piney sand. The vivid, hurrying ants were everywhere. To the squinted eye they looked like angry, orange ponies as they rode the pine needles. There was Geneva, skirting behind a tree, but she never came close or tried to get in the game. She pretended to be catching doodlebugs. The knife leaped and quivered in the sandy arena smoothed by Easter's hand.

'I may not know how to play, but I bet I win,' Jinny Love said.

Easter's eyes, lifting up, were neither brown nor green nor cat; they had something of metal, flat ancient metal, so that you could not see into them. Nina's grandfather had possessed a box of coins from Greece and Rome. Easter's eyes could have come from Greece or Rome that day. Jinny Love stopped short of apprehending this, and only took care to watch herself when Easter pitched the knife. The color in Easter's eyes could have been found somewhere, away – away, under lost leaves – strange as the painted color of the ants. Instead of round black holes in the center of her eyes, there might have been women's heads, ancient.

Easter, who had played so often, won. She nodded and accepted Jinny Love's barrette and from Nina a blue jay feather which she transferred to her own ear.

'I wouldn't be surprised if you cheated, and don't know what you had to lose if you lost,' said Jinny Love thoughtfully but with an admiration almost fantastic in her.

Victory with a remark attached did not crush Easter at all, or she scarcely listened. Her indifference made Nina fall back and listen to the spring running with an endless sound and see how the July light like purple and yellow birds kept flickering under the trees when the wind blew. Easter turned her head and the new feather on her head shone changeably. A black funnel of bees passed through the air, throwing a funneled shadow, like a visitor from nowhere, another planet.

'We have to play again to see whose the drinking cup will be,' Easter said, swaying forward on her knees.

Nina jumped to her feet and did a cartwheel. Against the spinning green and blue her heart pounded as heavily as she touched lightly.

'You ruined the game,' Jinny Love informed Easter. 'You don't know Nina.' She gathered up her cards. 'You'd think it was made of fourteen-carat gold, and didn't come out of the pocket of an old suitcase, that cup.'

'I'm sorry,' said Nina sincerely.

As the three were winding around the lake, a bird flying above the opposite shore kept uttering a cry and then diving deep, plunging into the trees there, and soaring to cry again.

'Hear him?' one of the Negroes said, fishing on the bank; it was Elberta's sister Twosie, who spoke as if a long, long conversation had been going on, into which she would intrude only the mildest words. 'Know why? Know why, in de sky, he say "Spirit? Spirit?" And den he dive *boom* and say "GHOST"?'

'Why does he?' said Jinny Love, in a voice of objection.

'Yawl knows. *I* don't know,' said Twosie, in her little high, helpless voice, and she shut her eyes. They couldn't seem to get on by her. On fine days there is danger of some sad meeting, the positive danger of it. '*I* don't know what he say dat for.' Twosie spoke pitifully, as though accused. She sighed. 'Yawl sho ain't got yo' eyes opem good, yawl. Yawl don't know what's out here in woods wid you.'

'Well, what?'

'Yawl walk right by mans wid great big gun, could jump out at yawl. Yawl don't eem smellim.'

'You mean Mr Holifield? That's a flashlight he's got.' Nina looked at Jinny Love for confirmation. Mr Holifield was their handy man, or rather simply 'the man to be sure and have around the camp.' He could be found by beating for a long time on the porch of the American Legion boat house – he slept heavily. 'He hasn't got a gun to jump out with.'

'I know who you mean. I hear those boys. Just some big boys, like the MacLain twins or somebody, and who cares about them?' Jinny Love, with her switch, indented the thick mat of hair on Twosie's head and prodded and stirred it gently. She pretended to fish in Twosie's woolly head. 'Why ain't *you* scared, then?'

'I is.'

Twosie's eyelids fluttered. Already she seemed to be fishing in her night's sleep. While they gazed at her crouched, devoted figure, from which the long pole hung, all their passions flew home again and went huddled and soft to roost.

Back at the camp, Jinny Love told Miss Moody about the great big jack-knife. Easter gave it up.

'I didn't mean you couldn't *drink* out of my cup,' Nina said, waiting for her. 'Only you have to hold it carefully, it leaks. It's engraved.'

Easter wouldn't even try it, though Nina dangled it on its ring right under her eyes. She didn't say anything, not even 'It's pretty.' Was she even thinking of it? Or if not, what did she think about?

'Sometimes orphans act like deaf-and-dumbs,' said Jinny Love.

III

'Nina!' Jinny Love whispered across the tent, during siesta. 'What do you think you're reading?'

Nina closed *The Re-Creation of Brian Kent*. Jinny Love was already coming directly across the almost-touching cots to Nina's, walking on her knees and bearing down over Gertrude, Etoile, and now Geneva.

With Jinny Love upon her, Geneva sighed. Her sleeping face looked as if she didn't want to. She slept as she swam, in her pantie-waist, she was in running position and her ribs went up and down frantically – a little box in her chest that expanded and shut without a second's rest between. Her cheek was pearly with afternoon moisture and her kitten-like teeth pearlier still. As Jinny Love hid her and went over, Nina seemed to see her still; even her vaccination mark looked too big for her.

Nobody woke up from being walked over, but after Jinny Love had fallen in bed with Nina, Easter gave a belated, dreaming sound. She had not even been in the line of march; she slept on the cot by the door, curved shell-like, both arms forward over her head. It was an inward sound she gave – now it came again – of such wholehearted and fateful concurrence with the thing dreamed, that Nina and Jinny Love took hands and made wry faces at each other.

Beyond Easter's cot the corona of afternoon flared and lifted in an intensity that came through the eyelids. There was nothing but light out there. True, the black Negroes inhabited it. Elberta moved slowly through it, as if she rocked a baby with her hips, carrying a bucket of scraps to throw in the lake – to get hail Columbia for it later. Her straw hat spiraled rings of orange and violet, like a top. Far, far down a vista of intolerable light, a tiny daub of black cotton, Twosie had stationed herself at the edge of things, and slept and fished.

Eventually there was Exum wandering with his fish pole – he could dance on a dime, Elberta said, he used to work for a blind man. Exum was smart for twelve years old; too smart. He found that hat he wore – not a sign of the owner. He had a hat like new, filled out a little with peanut shells inside the band to correct the size, and he like a little black peanut in it. It stood up and away from his head all around, and seemed only following him – on runners, perhaps, like those cartridges for change in Spights' store.

Easter's sighs and her prolonged or half-uttered words now filled the tent, just as the heat filled it. Her words fell in threes, Nina observed, like the mourning-dove's call in the woods.

Nina and Jinny Love lay speechless, doubling for themselves the already strong odor of Sweet Dreams Mosquito Oil, in a trance of endurance through the hour's siesta. Entwined, they stared -- orphan-like themselves – past Easter's cot and through the tent opening as down a long telescope turned on an incandescent star, and saw the spiral of Elberta's hat return, and saw Exum jump over a stick and on the other side do a little dance in a puff of dust. They could hear the intermittent crash, splash of Loch Morrison using their lake, and Easter's voice calling again in her sleep, her unintelligible words.

But however Nina and Jinny Love made faces at they knew not what, Easter concurred; she thoroughly agreed.

The bugle blew for swimming. Geneva jumped so hard she fell off her cot. Nina and Jinny Love were indented with each other, like pressed leaves, and jumped free. When Easter, who had to be shaken, sat up drugged and stupid on her cot, Nina ran over to her.

'Listen. Wake up. Look, you can go in in my bathing shoes today.'

She felt her eyes glaze with this plan of kindness as she stretched out her limp red shoes that hung down like bananas under Easter's gaze. But Easter dropped back on the cot and stretched her legs.

'Never mind your shoes. I don't have to go in the lake if I don't want to.'

'You do. I never heard of that. Who picked you out? You do,' they said, all gathering.

'You make me.'

Easter yawned. She fluttered her eyes and rolled them back – she loved doing that. Miss Moody passed by and beamed in at them hovered around Easter's passive and mutinous form. All along she'd been afraid of some challenge to her counselorship, from the way she hurried by now, almost too daintily.

'Well, *I* know,' Jinny Love said, sidling up. 'I know as much as you know, Easter.' She made a chant, which drove her hopping around the tent pole in an Indian step. 'You don't have to go, if you don't want to go. And if it ain't so, you still don't have to go, if you don't want to go.' She kissed her hand to them.

Easter was silent – but if she groaned when she waked, she'd only be imitating herself.

Jinny Love pulled on her bathing cap, which gave way and came down over her eyes. Even in blindness, she cried, 'So you needn't think you're the only one, Easter, not always. What do you say to that?'

'I should worry, I should cry,' said Easter, lying still, spread-eagled.

'Let's us run away from basket weaving,' Jinny Love said in Nina's ear, a little later in the week.

'Just as soon.'

'Grand. They'll think we're drowned.'

They went out the back end of the tent, barefooted; their feet were as tough as anybody's by this time. Down in the hammock, Miss Moody was reading *The Re-Creation of Brian Kent* now. (Nobody knew whose book that was, it had been found here, the covers curled up like side combs. Perhaps anybody at Moon Lake who tried to read it felt cheated by the title, as applying to camp life, as Nina did, and laid it down for the next person.) Cat, the cook's cat, was sunning on a post and when they approached jumped to the ground like something poured out of a bottle, and went with them, in front.

They trudged down the slope past Loch Morrison's

tent and took the track into the swamp. There they moved single file between two walls; by lifting their arms they could have touched one or the other pressing side of the swamp. Their toes exploded the dust that felt like the powder clerks pump into new kid gloves, as Jinny Love said twice. They were eye to eye with the finger-shaped leaves of the castor bean plants, put out like those gypsy hands that part the curtains at the back of rolling wagons, and wrinkled and coated over like the fortune-teller's face.

Mosquitoes struck at them; Sweet Dreams didn't last. The whining lifted like a voice, saying 'I don't want . . .' At the girls' shoulders Queen Anne's lace and elderberry and blackberry thickets, loaded heavily with flower and fruit and smelling with the melony smell of snake, over- hung the ditch to touch them. The ditches had dried green or blue bottoms, cracked and glazed – like a dropped vase. 'I hope we don't meet any boogerman,' Jinny Love said cheerfully.

Sweet bay and cypress and sweetgum and live oak and swamp maple closing tight made the wall dense, and yet there was somewhere still for the other wall of vine; it gathered itself on the ground and stacked and tilted itself in the trees; and like a table in the tree the mistletoe hung up there black in the zenith. Buzzards floated from one side of the swamp to the other, as if choice existed for them – raggedly crossing the sky and shadowing the track, and shouldering one another on the solitary limb of a moon-white sycamore. Closer to the ear than lips could begin words came the swamp sounds – closer to the ear and nearer to the dreaming mind. They were a song of hilarity to Jinny Love, who began to skip. Periods of silence seemed hoarse, or the suffering from hoarseness, otherwise inexplicable, as though the world could stop. Cat was stalking something at the black edge of the ditch. The briars didn't trouble Cat at all, it was they that seemed to give way beneath that long, boatlike belly.

The track serpentined again, and walking ahead was Easter. Geneva and Etoile were playing at her side, edging each other out of her shadow, but when they saw who was coming up behind them, they turned and ran tearing back towards camp, running at angles, like pullets, leaving a cloud of dust as they passed by.

'Wouldn't you know!' said Jinny Love.

Easter was going unconcernedly on, her dress stained green behind; she ate something out of her hand as she went.

'We'll soon catch up – don't hurry.'

The reason orphans were the way they were lay first in nobody's watching them, Nina thought, for she

felt obscurely like a trespasser. They, they were not answerable. Even on being watched, Easter remained not
answerable to a soul on earth. Nobody cared! And so, in
this beatific state, something came out of *her*.

'Where are you going?'

'Can we go with you, Easter?'

Easter, her lips stained with blackberries, replied, 'It
ain't my road.'

They walked along, one on each side of her. Though
they automatically stuck their tongues out at her, they
ran their arms around her waist. She tolerated the close-
ness for a little while; she smelled of orphan-starch, but
she had a strange pure smell of sweat, like a sleeping
baby, and in her temple, so close then to their eyes, the
skin was transparent enough for a little vein to be seen
pounding under it. She seemed very tender and very
small in the waist to be trudging along so doggedly,
when they had her like that.

Vines, a magnificent and steamy green, covered more
and more of the trees, played over them like fountains.
There were stretches of water below them, blue-black,
netted over with half-closed waterlilies. The horizontal
limbs of cypresses grew a short, pale green scruff like
bird feathers.

They came to a tiny farm down here, the last one
possible before the muck sucked it in – a patch of cotton

in flower, a house whitewashed in front, a cleanswept yard with a little iron pump standing in the middle of it like a black rooster. These were white people – an old woman in a sunbonnet came out of the house with a galvanized bucket, and pumped it full in the dooryard. That was an excuse to see people go by.

Easter, easing out of the others' clasp, lifted her arm halfway and, turning for an instant, gave two waves of the hand. But the old woman was prouder than she.

Jinny Love said, 'How would you all like to live there?'

Cat edged the woods onward, and at moments vanished into a tunnel in the briars. Emerging from other tunnels, he – or she – glanced up at them with a face more masklike than ever.

'There's a short-cut to the lake.' Easter, breaking and darting ahead, suddenly went down on her knees and slid under a certain place in the barbed-wire fence. Rising, she took a step inward, sinking down as she went. Nina untwined her arm from Jinny Love's and went after her.

'I might have known you'd want us to go through a barbed-wire fence.' Jinny Love sat down where she was, on the side of the ditch, just as she would take her seat on a needlepoint stool. She jumped up once, and sat back. 'Fools, fools!' she called. 'Now I think you've made me turn my ankle. Even if I wanted to track through the mud, I couldn't!'

Nina and Easter, dipping under a second, unexpected fence, went on, swaying and feeling their feet pulled down, reaching to the trees. Jinny Love was left behind in the heartless way people and incidents alike are thrown off in the course of a dream, like the gratuitous flowers scattered from a float – rather in celebration. The swamp was now all-enveloping, dark and at the same time vivid, alarming – it was like being inside the chest of something that breathed and might turn over.

Then there was Moon Lake, a different aspect altogether. Easter climbed the slight rise ahead and reached the pink, grassy rim and the innocent open. Here it was quiet, until, fatefully, there was one soft splash.

'You see the snake drop off in the water?' asked Easter.

'Snake?'

'Out of that tree.'

'You can have him.'

'There he is: coming up!' Easter pointed.

'That's probably a different one,' Nina objected in the voice of Jinny Love.

Easter looked both ways, chose, and walked on the pink sandy rim with its purpled lip, her blue shadow lolling over it. She went around a bend, and straight to an old gray boat. Did she know it would be there? It was in some reeds, looking mysterious to come upon and yet in place, as an old boat will. Easter stepped into it and hopped to the far seat that was over the water, and dropping to it lay back with her toes hooked up. She looked falling over backwards. One arm lifted, curved over her head, and hung till her finger touched the water.

The shadows of the willow leaves moved gently on the sand, deep blue and narrow, long crescents. The water was quiet, the color of pewter, marked with purple stobs, although where the sun shone right on it the lake seemed to be in violent agitation, almost boiling. Surely a little chip would turn around and around in it. Nina dropped down on the flecked sandbar. She fluttered her eyelids, half closed them, and the world looked struck by moonlight.

'Here I come,' came Jinny Love's voice. It hadn't been long. She came twitching over their tracks along the sandbar, her long soft hair blowing up like a skirt in a play of the breeze in the open. 'But I don't choose to sit myself in a leaky boat,' she was calling ahead. 'I choose the land.'

She took her seat on the very place where Nina was writing her name. Nina moved her finger away, drawing a long arrow to a new place. The sand was coarse like beads and full of minute shells, some shaped exactly like bugles.

'Want to hear about my ankle?' Jinny Love asked. 'It wasn't as bad as I thought. I must say you picked a queer place, I saw an *owl*. It smells like the school basement to me – peepee and old erasers.' Then she stopped with her mouth a little open, and was quiet, as though something had been turned off inside her. Her eyes were soft, her gaze stretched to Easter, to the boat, the lake – her long oval face went vacant.

Easter was lying rocked in the gentle motion of the boat, her head turned on its cheek. She had not said hello to Jinny Love anew. Did she see the drop of water clinging to her lifted finger? Did it make a rainbow? Not to Easter: her eyes were rolled back, Nina felt. Her own hand was writing in the sand. Nina, Nina, Nina. Writing, she could dream that her self might get away from her – that here in this faraway place she could tell her self, by name, to go or to stay. Jinny Love had begun building a sand castle over her foot. In the sky clouds moved no more perceptibly than grazing animals. Yet with a passing breeze, the boat gave a knock, lifted and fell. Easter sat up.

'Why aren't we out in the boat?' Nina, taking a strange and heady initiative, rose to her feet. 'Out there!' A picture in her mind, as if already furnished from an eventual and appreciative distance, showed the boat floating where she pointed, far out in Moon Lake with three girls sitting in the three spaces. 'We're coming, Easter!'

'Just as I make a castle. *I'm* not coming,' said Jinny Love. 'Anyway, there's stobs in the lake. We'd be upset, ha ha.'

'What do I care, I can swim!' Nina cried at the water's edge.

'You can just swim from the first post to the second post. And that's in front of camp, not here.'

Firming her feet in the sucking, minnowy mud, Nina put her weight against the boat. Soon her legs were half hidden, the mud like some awful kiss pulled at her toes, and all over she tautened and felt the sweat start out of her body. Roots laced her feet, knotty and streaming. Under water, the boat was caught too, but Nina was determined to free it. She saw that there was muddy water in the boat too, which Easter's legs, now bright pink, were straddling. Suddenly all seemed easy.

'It's coming loose!'

At the last minute, Jinny Love, who had extracted her foot from the castle with success, hurried over and climbed to the middle seat of the boat, screaming. Easter sat up swaying with the dip of the boat; the energy seemed all to have gone out of her. Her lolling head looked pale and featureless as a pear beyond the laughing face of Jinny Love. She had not said whether she wanted to go or not – yet surely she did; she had been in the boat all along, she had discovered the boat.

For a moment, with her powerful hands, Nina held the boat back. Again she thought of a pear – not the everyday gritty kind that hung on the tree in the back-yard, but the fine kind sold on trains and at high prices, each pear with a paper cone wrapping it alone – beautiful, symmetrical, clean pears with thin skins, with snow-white flesh so juicy and tender that to eat one baptized the whole face, and so delicate that while you urgently ate the first half, the second half was already beginning to turn brown. To all fruits, and especially to those fine pears, something happened – the process was so swift, you were never in time for them. It's not the flowers that are fleeting, Nina thought, it's the fruits – it's the time when things are ready that they don't stay. She even went through the rhyme, 'Pear tree by the garden gate, How much longer must I wait?' – thinking it was the pears that asked it, not the picker.

Then she climbed in herself, and they were rocking out sideways on the water.

'Now what?' said Jinny Love.

'This is all right for me,' said Nina.

'Without oars? – Ha ha.'

'Why didn't you tell me, then! – But I don't care now.'

'You never are as smart as you think.'

'Wait till you find out where we get to.'

'I guess you know Easter can't swim. She won't even touch water with her foot.'

'What do you think a *boat's* for?'

But a soft tug had already stopped their drifting. Nina with a dark frown turned and looked down.

'A chain! An old mean chain!'

'That's how smart you are.'

Nina pulled the boat in again – of course nobody helped her! – burning her hands on the chain, and kneeling outward tried to free the other end. She could see now through the reeds that it was wound around and around an old stump, which had almost grown over it in places. The boat had been chained to the bank since maybe last summer.

'No use hitting it,' said Jinny Love.

A dragonfly flew about their heads. Easter only waited in her end of the boat, not seeming to care about the disappointment either. If this was their ship, she was their figurehead, turned on its back, sky-facing. She wouldn't be their passenger.

'You thought we'd all be out in the middle of Moon

Lake by now, didn't you?' Jinny Love said, from her lady's seat. 'Well, look where we are.'

'Oh, Easter! Easter! I wish you still had your knife!'

'– But let's don't go back yet,' Jinny Love said on shore. 'I don't think they've missed me.' She started a sand castle over her other foot.

'You make me sick,' said Easter suddenly.

'Nina, let's pretend Easter's not with us.'

'But that's what *she* was pretending.'

Nina dug into the sand with a little stick, printing 'Nina' and then 'Easter.'

Jinny Love seemed stunned, she let sand run out of both fists. 'But how could you ever know what Easter was pretending?'

Easter's hand came down and wiped her name clean; she also wiped out 'Nina.' She took the stick out of Nina's hand and with a formal gesture, as if she would otherwise seem to reveal too much, wrote for herself. In clear, high-waisted letters the word 'Esther' cut into the sand. Then she jumped up.

'Who's that?' Nina asked.

Easter laid her thumb between her breasts, and walked about.

'Why, I call that "Esther."'

'Call it "Esther" if you want to, I call it "Easter." '

'Well, sit down . . .'

'And I named myself.'

'How could you? Who let you?'

'I let myself name myself.'

'Easter, I believe you,' said Nina. 'But I just want you to spell it right. Look – E-A-S –'

'I should worry, I should cry.'

Jinny Love leaned her chin on the roof of her castle to say, 'I was named for my maternal grandmother, so my name's Jinny Love. It couldn't be anything else. Or anything better. You see? Easter's just not a real name. It doesn't matter how she spells it, Nina, nobody ever had it. Not around here.' She rested on her chin.

'I have it.'

'Just see how it looks spelled right.' Nina lifted the stick from Easter's fingers and began to print, but had to throw herself bodily over the name to keep Easter from it. 'Spell it right and it's real!' she cried.

'But right or wrong, it's tacky,' said Jinny Love. 'You can't get me mad over it. All I can concentrate on out here is missing the figs at home.'

' "Easter" is real beautiful!' Nina said distractedly. She suddenly threw the stick into the lake, before Easter could grab it, and it trotted up and down in a crucible of sun-filled water. 'I thought it was the day you were

found on a doorstep,' she said sullenly – even distrust-
fully.

Easter sat down at last and with slow, careful move-
ments of her palms rubbed down the old bites on her
legs. Her crest of hair dipped downward and she rocked
a little, up and down, side to side, in a rhythm. Easter
never did intend to explain anything unless she had to –
or to force your explanations. She just had hopes. She
hoped never to be sorry. Or did she?

'I haven't got no father. I never had, he ran away. I've
got a mother. When I could walk, then my mother took
me by the hand and turned me in, and I remember it.
I'm going to be a singer.'

It was Jinny Love, starting to clear her throat, who
released Nina. It was Jinny Love, escaping, burrowing
her finger into her castle, who was now kind, pretending
Easter had never spoken. Nina banged Jinny Love on the
head with her fist. How good and hot her hair was! Like
hot glass. She broke the castle from her tender foot. She
wondered if Jinny Love's head would break. Not at all.
You couldn't learn anything through the head.

'Ha, ha, ha!' yelled Jinny Love, hitting back.

They were fighting and hitting for a moment. Then
they lay quiet, tilted together against the crumbled hill
of sand, stretched out and looking at the sky where
now a white tower of cloud was climbing.

Someone moved; Easter lifted to her lips a piece of cross-vine cut back in the days of her good knife. She brought up a kitchen match from her pocket, lighted up, and smoked.

They sat up and gazed at her.

'If you count much on being a singer, that's not a very good way to start,' said Jinny Love. 'Even boys, it stunts their growth.'

Easter once more looked the same as asleep in the dancing shadows, except for what came out of her mouth, more mysterious, almost, than words.

'Have some?' she asked, and they accepted. But theirs went out.

Jinny Love's gaze was fastened on Easter, and she dreamed and dreamed of telling on her for smoking, while the sun, even through leaves, was burning her pale skin pink, and she looked the most beautiful of all: she felt temptation. But what she said was, 'Even after all this is over, Easter, I'll always remember you.'

Off in the thick of the woods came a fairy sound, fol-lowed by a tremulous silence, a holding apart of the air.

'What's that?' cried Easter sharply. Her throat quiv-ered, the little vein in her temple jumped.

'That's Mister Loch Morrison. Didn't you know he had a horn?'

There was another fairy sound, and the pried-apart, gentle silence. The woods seemed to be moving after it, running – the world pellmell. Nina could see the boy in the distance, too, and the golden horn tilted up. A few minutes back her gaze had fled the present and this scene; now she put the horn blower into his visionary place.

'Don't blow that!' Jinny Love cried out this time, jumping to her feet and stopping up her ears, stamping on the shore of Moon Lake. 'You shut up! We can hear! – Come on,' she added prosaically to the other two. 'It's time to go. I reckon they've worried enough.' She smiled. 'Here comes Cat.'

Cat always caught something; something was in his – or her – mouth, a couple of little feet or claws bouncing under the lifted whiskers. Cat didn't look especially triumphant; just through with it.

They marched on away from their little boat.

IV

One clear night the campers built a fire up above the spring, cooked supper on sticks around it, and after stunts, a recitation of 'How They Brought the Good News from Ghent to Aix' by Gertrude Bowles, and the ghost story about the bone, they stood up on the ridge and poured a last song into the woods – 'Little Sir Echo.'

The fire was put out and there was no bright point to look into, no circle. The presence of night was beside them – a beast in gossamer, with no shine of outline, only of ornament – rings, earrings . . .

'March!' cried Mrs Gruenwald, and stamped down the trail for them to follow. They went single file on the still-warm pine needles, soundlessly now. Not far away there were crackings of twigs, small, regretted crashes; Loch Morrison, supperless for all they knew, was wandering around by himself, sulking, alone.

Nobody needed light. The night sky was pale as a green grape, transparent like grape flesh over each tree. Every girl saw moths – the beautiful ones like ladies, with long legs that were wings – and the little ones, mere bits of bark. And once against the night, just before Little Sister Spights' eyes, making her cry out, hung suspended a spider – a body no less mysterious than the grape of the air, different only a little.

All around swam the fireflies. Clouds of them, trees of them, islands of them floating, a lower order of brightness – one could even get into a tent by mistake. The stars barely showed their places in the pale sky – small and far from this bright world. And the world would be bright as long as these girls held awake, and could keep their eyes from closing. And the moon itself shone – taken for granted.

Moon Lake came in like a flood below the ridge; they trailed downward. Out there Miss Moody would sometimes go in a boat; sometimes she had a late date from town, 'Rudy' Spights or 'Rudy' Loomis, and then they could be seen drifting there after the moon was up, far out on the smooth bright surface. ('And she lets him hug her out there,' Jinny Love had instructed them. 'Like this.' She had seized, of all people, Etoile, whose name rhymed with tinfoil. 'Hands off,' said Etoile.) Twice Nina had herself seen the silhouette of the canoe on the bright water, with the figures at each end, like a dark butterfly with wings spread open and still. Not tonight!

Tonight, it was only the helpers, fishing. But their boat must be full of silver fish! Nina wondered if it was the slowness and near-fixity of boats out on the water that made them so magical. Their little boat in the reeds that day had not been far from this one's wonder, after all. The turning of water and sky, of the moon, or the sun, always proceeded, and there was this magical hesitation in their midst, of a boat. And in the boat, it was not so much that they drifted, as that in the presence of a boat the world drifted, forgot. The dreamed-about changed places with the dreamer.

Home from the wild moonlit woods, the file of little girls wormed into the tents, which were hot as cloth pockets. The candles were lighted by Miss Moody, dateless tonight, on whose shelf in the flare of nightly revelation stood her toothbrush in the glass, her handpainted celluloid powder box, her Honey and Almond cream, her rouge and eyebrow tweezers, and at the end of the line the bottle of Compound, containing true and false unicorn and the life root plant.

Miss Moody, with a fervent frown which precluded interruption, sang in soft tremolo as she rubbed the lined-up children with 'Sweet Dreams.'

> 'Forgive me
> O please forgive me
> I didn't mean to make
> You cry!
> I love you and I need you –'

They crooked and bent themselves and lifted nightgowns to her silently while she sang. Then when she faced them to her they could look into the deep tangled rats of her puffed hair and at her eyebrows which seemed fixed for ever in that elevated line of adult pleading.

'Do anything but don't say good-bye!'

And automatically they almost said, 'Good-bye!' Her hands rubbed and cuffed them while she sang, pulling to her girls all just alike, as if girlhood itself were an infinity, but a commodity. ('I'm ticklish,' Jinny Love informed her every night.) Her look of pleading seemed infinitely perilous to them. Her voice had the sway of an aerialist crossing the high wire, even while she sang out of the nightgown coming down over her head.

There were kisses, prayers. Easter, as though she could be cold tonight, got into bed with Geneva. Geneva like a little June bug hooked onto her back. The candles were blown. Miss Moody ostentatiously went right to sleep. Jinny Love cried into her pillow for her mother, or perhaps for the figs. Just outside their tent, Citronella burned in a saucer in the weeds – Citronella, like a girl's name.

Luminous of course but hidden from them, Moon Lake streamed out in the night. By moonlight sometimes it seemed to run like a river. Beyond the cry of the frogs there were the sounds of a boat moored somewhere, of its vague, clumsy reaching at the shore, those sounds that are recognized as being made by something sightless. When did boats have eyes – once? Nothing watched that their little part of the lake stayed roped off and protected; was it there now, the rope stretched frail-like between posts that swayed in mud? That rope was to mark how far the girls could swim. Beyond lay the deep part, some bottomless parts, said Moody. Here and there was the quicksand that stirred your footprint and kissed your heel. All snakes, harmless and harmful, were freely playing now; they put a trailing, moony division between weed and weed – bright, turning, bright and turning.

Nina still lay dreamily, or she had waked in the night. She heard Gertrude Bowles gasp in a dream, beginning to get her stomach ache, and Etoile begin, slowly, her snore. She thought: Now I can think, in between them. She could not even feel Miss Moody fretting.

The orphan! she thought exultantly. The other way to live. There were secret ways. She thought, Time's really short, I've been only thinking like the others. It's only interesting, only worthy, to try for the fiercest secrets. To slip into them all – to change. To change for a moment into Gertrude, into Mrs Gruenwald, into Twosie – into a boy. To *have been* an orphan.

Nina sat up on the cot and stared passionately before

her at the night – the pale dark roaring night with its secret step, the Indian night. She felt the forehead, the beaded stars, look in thoughtfully at her.

The pondering night stood rude at the tent door, the opening fold would let it stoop in – it, him – he had risen up inside. Long-armed, or long-winged, he stood in the center there where the pole went up. Nina lay back, drawn quietly from him. But the night knew about Easter. All about her. Geneva had pushed her to the very edge of the cot. Easter's hand hung down, opened outward. Come here, night, Easter might say, tender to a giant, to such a dark thing. And the night, obedient and graceful, would kneel to her. Easter's callused hand hung open there to the night that had got wholly into the tent.

Nina let her own arm stretch forward opposite Easter's. Her hand too opened, of itself. She lay there a long time motionless, under the night's gaze, its black cheek, looking immovably at her hand, the only part of her now which was not asleep. Its gesture was like Easter's, but Easter's hand slept and her own hand knew – shrank and knew, yet offered still.

'Instead . . . me instead . . .'

In the cup of her hand, in her filling skin, in the fingers' bursting weight and stillness, Nina felt it: compassion and a kind of competing that were all one, a single ecstasy, a single longing. For the night was not impartial. No, the night loved some more than others, served some more than others. Nina's hand lay open there for a long time, as if its fingers would be its eyes. Then it too slept. She dreamed her hand was helpless to the tearing teeth of wild beasts. At reveille she woke up lying on it. She could not move it. She hit it and bit it until like a cluster of bees it stung back and came to life.

V

They had seen, without any idea of what he would do – and yet it was just like him – little old Exum toiling up the rough barky ladder and dreaming it up, clinging there monkeylike among the leaves, all eyes and wrinkled forehead.

Exum was apart too, boy and colored to boot; he constantly moved along an even further fringe of the landscape than Loch, wearing the man's stiff straw hat brilliant as a snowflake. They would see Exum in the hat bobbing along the rim of the swamp like a fisherman's cork, elevated just a bit by the miasma and illusion of the landscape he moved in. It was Exum persistent as a little bug, inching along the foot of the swamp wall, carrying around a fishing cane and minnow can, fishing

around the bend from their side of the lake, catching all
kinds of things. Things, things. He claimed all he
caught, gloating – dangled it and loved it, clasped it with
suspicious glee – wouldn't a soul dispute him that? The
Boy Scout asked him if he could catch an electric eel
and Exum promised it readily – a gift; the challenge was
a siesta-long back-and-forth across the water.

Now all rolling eyes, he hung on the ladder, too little
to count as looking – too everything-he-was to count as
anything.

Beyond him on the diving-board, Easter was standing –
high above the others at their swimming lesson. She
was motionless, barefooted, and tall with her outgrown,
printed dress on her and the sky under her. She had
not answered when they called things up to her. They
splashed noisily under her callused, coral-colored foot
that hung over.

'How are you going to get down, Easter!' shouted
Gertrude Bowles.

Miss Moody smiled understandingly up at Easter.
How far, in the water, could Miss Parnell Moody be
transformed from a schoolteacher? They had wondered. She wore a canary yellow bathing cap lumpy
over her hair, with a rubber butterfly on the front. She
wore a brassiere and bloomers under her bathing suit
because, said Jinny Love, that was exactly how good she

43

was. She scarcely looked for trouble, immediate trouble –
though this was the last day at Moon Lake.

Exum's little wilted black fingers struck at his lips as
if playing a tune on them. He put out a foolishly long
arm. He held a green willow switch. Later they every
one said they saw him – but too late. He gave Easter's
heel the tenderest, obscurest little brush, with something of nigger persuasion about it.

She dropped like one hit in the head by a stone from
a sling. In their retrospect, her body, never turning,
seemed to languish upright for a moment, then descend.
It went to meet and was received by blue air. It dropped
as if handed down all the way and was let into the brown
water almost on Miss Moody's crown, and went out of
sight at once. There was something so positive about its
disappearance that only the instinct of caution made
them give it a moment to come up again; it didn't come
up. Then Exum let loose a girlish howl and clung to the
ladder as though a fire had been lighted under it.

Nobody called for Loch Morrison. On shore, he stu-
diously hung his bugle on the tree. He was enormously
barefooted. He took a frog dive and when he went
through the air they noticed that the powdered-on dirt
gave him lavender soles. Now he swam destructively
into the water, cut through the girls, and began to hunt
Easter where all the fingers began to point.

They cried while he hunted, their chins dropping into the brown buggy stuff and their mouths sometimes swallowing it. He didn't give a glance their way. He stayed under as though the lake came down a lid on him, at each dive. Sometimes, open-mouthed, he appeared with something awful in his hands, showing not them, but the world, or himself – long ribbons of green and terrible stuff, shapeless black matter, nobody's shoe. Then he would up-end and go down, hunting her again. Each dive was a call on Exum to scream again.

'Shut up! Get out of the way! You stir up the lake!' Loch Morrison yelled once – blaming them. They looked at one another and after one loud cry all stopped crying. Standing in the brown that cut them off where they waited, ankle-deep, waist-deep, knee-deep, chin-deep, they made a little V, with Miss Moody in front and partly obscuring their vision with her jerky butterfly cap. They felt his insult. They stood so still as to be almost carried away, in the pictureless warm body of lake around them, until they felt the weight of the currentless water pulling anyhow. Their shadows only, like the curled back edges of a split drum, showed where they each protruded out of Moon Lake.

Up above, Exum howled, and further up, some fulsome, vague clouds with uneasy hearts blew peony-like. Exum howled up, down, and all around. He brought

Elberta, mad, from the cook tent, and surely Mrs Gruenwald was dead to the world – asleep or reading – or she
would be coming too, by now, capering down her
favorite trail. It was Jinny Love, they realized, who had
capered down, and now stood strangely signaling from
shore. The painstaking work of Miss Moody, white
bandages covered her arms and legs; poison ivy had
appeared that morning. Like Easter, Jinny Love had no
intention of going in the lake.

'Ahhhhh!' everybody said, long and drawn out, just
as he found her.

Of course he found her, there was her arm sliding
through his hand. They saw him snatch the hair of
Easter's head, the way a boy will snatch anything he
wants, as if he won't have invisible opponents snatching
first. Under the water he joined himself to her. He
spouted, and with engine-like jerks brought her in.

There came Mrs Gruenwald. With something like a
skip, she came to a stop on the bank and waved her
hands. Her middy blouse flew up, showing her loosened
corset. It was red. They treasured that up. But her voice
was pre-emptory.

'This minute! Out of the lake! Out of the lake, out-
out! Parnell! Discipline! March them out.'

'One's drowned!' shrieked poor Miss Moody.

Loch stood over Easter. He sat her up, folding, on the shore, wheeled her arm over, and by that dragged her clear of the water before he dropped her, a wrapped bundle in the glare. He shook himself in the sun like a dog, blew his nose, spat, and shook his ears, all in a kind of leisurely trance that kept Mrs Gruenwald off – as though he had no notion that he was interrupting things at all. Exum could now be heard shrieking for Miss Marybelle Steptoe, the lady who had had the camp last year and was now married and living in the Delta.

Miss Moody and all her girls now came out of the lake. Tardy, drooping, their hair heavy-wet and their rubber shoes making wincing sounds, they edged the shore.

Loch returned to Easter, spread her out, and then they could all get at her, but they watched the water lake in her lap. The sun like a weight fell on them. Miss Moody wildly ran and caught up Easter's ankle and pushed on her, like a lady with a wheelbarrow. The Boy Scout looped Easter's arms like sashes on top of her and took up his end, the shoulders. They carried her, looking for shade. One arm fell, touching ground. Jinny Love, in the dazzling bandages, ran up and scooped Easter's arm in both of hers. They proceeded, zigzag, Jinny Love turning her head toward the rest of them, running low, bearing the arm.

They put her down in the only shade on earth, after all, the table under the tree. It was where they ate. The table was itself still mostly tree, as the ladder and diving board were half tree too; a camp table had to be round and barky on the underside, and odorous of having been chopped down. They knew that splintery surface, and the ants that crawled on it. Mrs Gruenwald, with her strong cheeks, blew on the table, but she might have put a cloth down. She stood between table and girls; her tennis shoes, like lesser corsets, tied her feet solid there; and they did not go any closer, but only to where they could see.

'I got her, please ma'am.'

In the water, the life saver's face had held his whole impatience; now it was washed pure, blank. He pulled Easter his way, away from Miss Moody – who, however, had got Easter's sash ends wrung out – and then, with a turn, hid her from Mrs Gruenwald. Holding her folded up to him, he got her clear, and the next moment, with a spread of his hand, had her lying there before him on the table top.

They were silent. Easter lay in a mold of wetness from Moon Lake, on her side; sharp as a flatiron her hipbone pointed up. She was arm to arm and leg to leg in a long fold, wrong-colored and pressed together as unopen leaves are. Her breasts, too, faced together. Out of the water Easter's hair was darkened, and lay over her face in long fern shapes. Miss Moody laid it back.

'You can tell she's not breathing,' said Jinny Love.

Easter's nostrils were pinched-looking like an old country woman's. Her side fell slack as a dead rabbit's in the woods, with the flowers of her orphan dress all running together in some antic of their own, some belated mix-up of the event. The Boy Scout had only let her go to leap onto the table with her. He stood over her, put his hands on her, and rolled her over; they heard the distant-like knock of her forehead on the solid table, and the knocking of her hip and knee.

Exum was heard being whipped in the willow clump; then they remembered Elberta was his mother. 'You little black son-a-bitch!' they heard her yelling, and he howled through the woods.

Astride Easter the Boy Scout lifted her up between his legs and dropped her. He did it again, and she fell on one arm. He nodded – not to them.

There was a sigh, a Morgana sigh, not an orphans'. The orphans did not press forward, or claim to own or protect Easter any more. They did nothing except mill a little, and yet their group was delicately changed. In Nina's head, where the world was still partly leisurely, came a recollected scene: birds on a roof under a cherry tree; they were drunk.

The Boy Scout, nodding, took Easter's hair and turned her head. He left her face looking at them. Her eyes were neither open nor altogether shut but as if her ears heard a great noise, back from the time she fell; the whites showed under the lids pale and slick as watermelon seeds. Her lips were parted to the same degree, her teeth could be seen smeared with black mud.

The Boy Scout reached in and gouged out her mouth with his hand, an unbelievable act. She did not alter. He lifted up, screwed his toes, and with a groan of his own fell upon her and drove up and down upon her, into her, gouging the heels of his hands into her ribs again and again. She did not alter except that she let a thin stream of water out of her mouth, a dark stain down the fixed cheek. The children drew together. Life-saving was much worse than they had dreamed. Worse still was the carelessness of Easter's body.

Jinny Love volunteered once more. She would wave a towel over things to drive the mosquitoes, at least, away. She chose a white towel. Her unspotted arms lifted and criss-crossed. She faced them now; her expression quietened and became ceremonious.

Easter's body lay up on the table to receive anything that was done to it. If *he* was brutal, her self, her body, the withheld life, was brutal too. While the Boy Scout as if he rode a runaway horse clung momently to her and arched himself off her back, dug his knees and fists into her and was flung back careening by his own tactics, she lay there.

Let him try and try!

The next thing Nina knew was a scent of home, an adult's thumb in her shoulder, and a cry, 'Now what?' Miss Lizzie Stark pushed in front of her, where her hips and black purse swung to a full stop, blotting out everything. She was Jinny Love's mother and had arrived on her daily visit to see how the camp was running.

They never heard the electric car coming, but usually they saw it, watched for it in the landscape, as out of place as a piano rocking over the holes and taking the bumps, making a high wall of dust.

Nobody dared tell Miss Lizzie; only Loch Morrison's grunts could be heard.

'Some orphan get too much of it?' Then she said more loudly, 'But what's *he* doing to her? Stop that.'

The Morgana girls all ran to her and clung to her skirt.

'Get off me,' she said. 'Now look here, everybody. I've got a weak heart. You all know that. – Is that *Jinny Love*?'

'Leave me alone, Mama,' said Jinny Love, waving the towel.

Miss Lizzie, whose hands were on Nina's shoulders,

shook Nina. 'Jinny Love Stark, come here to me, Loch Morrison, get off that table and shame on you.'

Miss Moody was the one brought to tears. She walked up to Miss Lizzie holding a towel in front of her breast and weeping. 'He's our life saver, Miss Lizzie. Remember? Our Boy Scout. Oh, mercy, I'm thankful you've come, he's been doing that a long time. Stand in the shade, Miss Lizzie.'

'Boy Scout? Why, he ought to be – he ought to be – I can't stand it, Parnell Moody.'

'Can't any of us help it, Miss Lizzie. Can't any of us. It's what he came for.' She wept.

'That's Easter,' Geneva said. 'That is.'

'He ought to be put out of business,' Miss Lizzie Stark said. She stood in the center of them all, squeezing Nina uncomfortably for Jinny Love, who flouted her up in front, and Nina could look up at her. The white rice powder which she used on the very front of her face twinkled on her faint mustache. She smelled of red pepper and lemon juice – she had been making them some mayonnaise. She was valiantly trying to make up for all the Boy Scout was doing by what she was thinking of him: that he was odious. Miss Lizzie's carelessly flung word to him on sight – the first day – had been, 'You little rascal, I bet you run down and pollute the spring, don't you?' 'Nome,' the Boy Scout had said, showing the first evidence of his gloom.

'Tears won't help, Parnell,' Miss Lizzie said. 'Though some don't know what tears are.' She glanced at Mrs Gruenwald, who glanced back from another level; she had brought herself out a chair. 'And our last afternoon. I'd thought we'd have a treat.'

They looked around as here came Marvin, Miss Lizzie's yard boy, holding two watermelons like a mother with twins. He came toward the table and just stood there.

'Marvin. You can put those melons down, don't you see the table's got somebody on it?' Miss Lizzie said. 'Put 'em down and wait.'

Her presence made this whole happening seem more in the nature of things. They were glad Miss Lizzie had come! It was somehow for this that they had given those yells for Miss Lizzie as Camp Mother. Under her gaze the Boy Scout's actions seemed to lose a good deal of significance. He was reduced almost to a nuisance – a mosquito, with a mosquito's proboscis. 'Get him off her,' Miss Lizzie repeated, in her rich and yet careless, almost humorous voice, knowing it was no good. 'Ah, get him off her.' She stood hugging the other little girls, several of them, warmly. Her gaze only hardened on Jinny Love; they hugged her all the more.

She loved them. It seemed the harder it was to get out here and the harder a time she found them having, the better she appreciated them. They remembered now – while the Boy Scout still drove up and down on Easter's muddy back – how they were always getting ready for Miss Lizzie; the tents even now were straight and the ground picked up and raked for her, and the tea for supper was already made and sitting in a tub in the lake; and sure enough, the Negroes' dog had barked at the car just as always, and now here she was. She could have stopped everything; and she hadn't stopped it. Even her opening protests seemed now like part of things – what she was supposed to say. Several of the little girls looked up at Miss Lizzie instead of at what was on the table. Her powdered lips flickered, her eyelids hooded her gaze, but she was there.

On the table, the Boy Scout spat, and took a fresh appraisal of Easter. He reached for a hold on her hair and pulled her head back. No longer were her lips faintly parted – her mouth was open. It gaped. So did his. He dropped her, the head with its suddenness bowed again on its cheek, and he started again.

'Easter's dead! Easter's d—' cried Gertrude Bowles in a rowdy voice, and she was slapped rowdily across the mouth to cut off the word, by Miss Lizzie's hand.

Jinny Love, with a persistence they had not dreamed of, deployed the towel. Could it be owing to Jinny Love's always being on the right side that Easter mustn't dare die and bring all this to a stop? Nina thought, It's I that's thinking. Easter's not thinking at all. And while not thinking, she is not dead, but unconscious, which is even harder to be. Easter had come among them and had held herself untouchable and intact. Of course, for one little touch could smirch her, make her fall so far, so deep. – Except that by that time they were all saying the nigger deliberately poked her off in the water, meant her to drown.

'Don't touch her,' they said tenderly to one another.

'Give up! Give up! Give up!' screamed Miss Moody – she who had rubbed them all the same, as if she rubbed chickens for the frying pan. Miss Lizzie without hesitation slapped her too.

'Don't touch her.'

For they were crowding closer to the table all the time.

'If Easter's dead, I get her coat for winter, all right,' said Geneva.

'Hush, orphan.'

'Is she then?'

'You shut up.' The Boy Scout looked around and panted at Geneva. 'You can ast *me* when I ast you to ast me.'

*

The dog was barking again. Other dogs barked back.

'Now who?'

'A big boy. It's old Ran MacLain and he's coming.'

'He would.'

He came right up, wearing a cap.

'Get away from me, Ran MacLain,' Miss Lizzie called toward him. 'You and dogs and guns, keep away. We've already got all we can put up with out here.'

She put her foot down on his asking any questions, getting up on the table, or leaving, now that he'd come. Under his cap bill, Ran MacLain set his gaze – he was twenty-three, his seasoned gaze – on Loch and Easter on the table. He could not be prevented from considering them all. He moved under the tree. He held his gun under his arm. He let two dogs run loose, and almost imperceptibly, he chewed gum. Only Miss Moody did not move away from him.

And pressing closer to the table, Nina almost walked into Easter's arm flung out over the edge. The arm was turned at the elbow so that the hand opened upward. It held there the same as it had held when the night came in and stood in the tent, when it had come to Easter and not to Nina. It was the one hand, and it seemed the one moment.

'Don't touch her.'

Nina fainted. She woke up to the cut-onion odor of

Elberta's underarm. She was up on the table with Easter, foot to head. There was so much she loved at home, but there was only time to remember the front yard. The silver, sweet-smelling paths strewed themselves behind the lawn mower, the four-o'clocks blazed. Then Elberta raised her up, she got down from the table, and was back with the others.

'Keep away. Keep away, I told you you better keep away. Leave me alone,' Loch Morrison was saying with short breaths. 'I dove for her, didn't I?'

They hated him, Nina most of all. Almost, they hated Easter.

They looked at Easter's mouth and at the eyes where they were contemplating without sense the back side of the light. Though she had bullied and repulsed them earlier, they began to speculate in another kind of allurement: was there danger that Easter, turned in on herself, might call out to them after all, from the other, worse, side of it? Her secret voice, if soundless then possibly visible, might work out of her terrible mouth like a vine, preening and sprung with flowers. Or a snake would come out.

The Boy Scout crushed in her body and blood came out of her mouth. For them all, it was like being spoken to.

'Nina, you! Come stand right here in my skirt,' Miss Lizzie called. Nina went and stood under the big bosom that started down, at the neck of her dress, like a big cloven white hide.

Jinny Love was catching her mother's eye. Of course she had stolen brief rests, but now her white arms lifted the white towel and whipped it bravely. She looked at them until she caught their eye – as if in the end the party was for *her*.

Marvin had gone back to the car and brought two more melons, which he stood holding.

'Marvin. We aren't ready for our watermelon. I told you.'

'Oh, Ran. How could you? Oh, Ran.'

That was Miss Moody in still a third manifestation.

By now the Boy Scout seemed for ever part of Easter and she part of him, he in motion on the up-and-down and she stretched across. He was dripping, while her skirt dried on the table; so in a manner they had changed places too. Was time moving? Endlessly, Ran MacLain's dogs frisked and played, with the Negroes' dog between.

Time was moving because in the beginning Easter's face – the curve of her brow, the soft upper lip and the milky eyes – partook of the swoon of her fall – the almost forgotten fall that bathed her so purely in blue for that long moment. The face was set now, and ugly with that rainy color of seedling petunias, the kind nobody wants. Her mouth surely by now had been open long enough, as long as any gape, bite, cry, hunger, satisfaction lasts, any one person's grief, or even protest.

Not all the children watched, and their heads all were beginning to hang, to nod. Everybody had forgotten about crying. Nina had spotted three little shells in the sand she wanted to pick up when she could. And suddenly this seemed to her one of those moments out of the future, just as she had found one small brief one out of the past; this was far, far ahead of her – picking up the shells, one, another, another, without time moving any more, and Easter abandoned on a little edifice, beyond dying and beyond being remembered about.

'I'm so tired!' Gertrude Bowles said. 'And hot. Ain't you tired of Easter, laying up there on that table?'

'My arms are about to break, you all,' and Jinny Love stood and hugged them to her.

'I'm so tired of Easter,' Gertrude said.

'Wish she'd go ahead and die and get it over with,' said Little Sister Spights, who had been thumb-sucking all afternoon without a reprimand.

'I give up,' said Jinny Love.

Miss Lizzie beckoned, and she came. 'I and Nina and Easter all went out in the woods, and I was the only one that came back with poison ivy,' she said, kissing her mother.

Miss Lizzie sank her fingers critically into the arms of the girls at her skirt. They all rose on tiptoe. Was Easter dead then?

Looking out for an instant from precarious holds, they took in sharply for memory's sake that berated figure, the mask formed and set on the face, one hand displayed, one jealously clawed under the waist, as if a secret handful had been groveled for, the spread and spotted legs. It was a betrayed figure, the betrayal was over, it was a memory. And then as the blows, automatic now, swung down again, the figure itself gasped.

'Get back. Get back.' Loch Morrison spoke between cruel, gritted teeth to them, and crouched over.

And when they got back, her toes webbed outward. Her belly arched and drew up from the board under her. She fell, but she kicked the Boy Scout.

Ridiculously, he tumbled backwards off the table. He fell almost into Miss Lizzie's skirt; she halved herself on the instant, and sat on the ground with her lap spread out before her like some magnificent hat that has just got crushed. Ran MacLain hurried politely over to pick her up, but she fought him off.

'Why don't you go home – now!' she said.

Before their eyes, Easter got to her knees, sat up, and drew her legs up to her. She rested her head on her knees and looked out at them, while she slowly pulled her ruined dress downward.

The sun was setting. They felt it directly behind them, the warmth flat as a hand. Easter leaned slightly over the table's edge, as if to gaze down at what might move, and blew her nose; she accomplished that with the aid of her finger, like people from away in the country. Then she sat looking out again; in another moment her legs dropped and hung down. The girls looked back at her, through the yellow and violet streams of dust – just now reaching them from Ran MacLain's flivver – the air coarse as sacking let down from the tree branches. Easter lifted one arm and shaded her eyes, but the arm fell in her lap like a clod.

There was a sighing sound from them. For the first time they noticed there was an old basket on the table. It held their knives, forks, tin cups and plates.

'Carry me.' Easter's words had no inflection. Again, 'Carry me.'

She held out her arms to them, stupidly.

Then Ran MacLain whistled to his dogs.

The girls ran forward all together. Mrs Gruenwald's fists rose in the air as if she lifted – no, rather, had lowered – a curtain and she began with a bleating sound, 'Pa-a-ack –'

'–up your troubles in your old kit bag
And smile, smile, smile!'

The Negroes were making a glorious commotion,
all of them came up now, and then Exum escaped them
all and ran waving away to the woods, dainty as a loosened rabbit.

'Who was he, that big boy?' Etoile was asking Jinny
Love.

'Ran MacLain, slow-poke.'

'What did he want?'

'He's just waiting on the camp. *They're* coming out
tomorrow, hunting. I heard all he said to Miss Moody.'

'Did Miss Moody *know* him?'

'Anybody knows him, and his twin brother too.'

Nina, running up in the front line with the others,
sighed – the sigh she gave when she turned in her exam-
ination papers at school. Then with each step she felt a
defiance of her own. She screamed, 'Easter!'

In that passionate instant, when they reached Easter
and took her up, many feelings returned to Nina, some
joining and some conflicting. At least what had happened to Easter was out in the world, like the table
itself. There it remained – mystery, if only for being
hard and cruel and, by something Nina felt inside her
body, murderous.

Now they had Easter and carried her up to the tent, Mrs Gruenwald still capering backwards and leading on,

'–in your old kit bag!
Smile, girls-instead-of-boys, that's the style!'

Miss Lizzie towered along darkly, groaning. She grabbed hold of Little Sister Spights, and said, 'Can *you* brush me off!' She would be taking charge soon, but for now she asked for a place to sit down and a glass of cold water. She did not speak to Marvin yet; he was shoving the watermelons up onto the table.

Their minds could hardly capture it again, the way Easter was standing free in space, then handled and turned over by the blue air itself. Some of them looked back and saw the lake, rimmed around with its wall-within-walls of woods, into which the dark had already come. There were the water wings of Little Sister Spights, floating yet, white as a bird. 'I know another Moon Lake,' one girl had said yesterday. 'Oh, my child, Moon Lakes are all over the world,' Mrs Gruenwald had interrupted. 'I know of one in Austria . . .' And into each fell a girl, they dared, now, to think.

The lake grew darker, then gleamed, like the water of a rimmed well. Easter was put to bed, they sat quietly on the ground outside the tent, and Miss Lizzie sipped water from Nina's cup. The sky's rising clouds lighted all over, like one spread-out blooming mimosa tree that could be seen from where the trunk itself should rise.

VI

Nina and Jinny Love, wandering down the lower path with arms entwined, saw the Boy Scout's tent. It was after the watermelon feast, and Miss Lizzie's departure. Miss Moody, in voile and tennis shoes, had a date with old 'Rudy' Loomis, and Mrs Gruenwald was trying to hold the girls with a sing before bedtime. Easter slept; Twosie watched her.

Nina and Jinny Love could hear the floating songs, farewell-like, the cheers and yells between. An owl hooted in a tree, closer by. The wind stirred.

On the other side of the tent wall the slats of the Boy Scout's legs shuttered open and shut like a fan when he moved back and forth. He had a lantern in there, or perhaps only a candle. He finished off his own shadow by opening the flap of his tent. Jinny Love and Nina halted on the path, quiet as old campers.

The Boy Scout, little old Loch Morrison, was undressing in his tent for the whole world to see. He took his time wrenching off each garment; then he threw it to the floor as hard as he would throw a ball; yet that seemed, in him, meditative.

His candle – for that was all it was – jumping a little now, he stood there studying and touching his case of sunburn in a Kress mirror like theirs. He was naked and there was his little tickling thing hung on him like the last drop on the pitcher's lip. He ceased or exhausted study and came to the tent opening again and stood leaning on one raised arm, with his weight on one foot – just looking out into the night, which was clamorous.

It seemed to them he had little to do!

Hadn't he surely, just before they caught him, been pounding his chest with his fists? Bragging on himself? It seemed to them they could still hear in the beating air of night the wild tattoo of pride he must have struck off. His silly, brief, overriding little show they could well imagine there in his tent of separation in the middle of the woods, in the night. Minnowy thing that matched his candle flame, naked as he was with that, he thought he shone forth too. Didn't he?

Nevertheless, standing there with the tent slanting over him and his arm knobby as it reached up and his head bent a little, he looked rather at loose ends.

'We can call like an owl,' Nina suggested. But Jinny Love thought in terms of the future. 'I'll tell on him, in Morgana tomorrow. He's the most conceited Boy Scout in the whole troop; and's bowlegged.

'You and I will always be old maids,' she added.

Then they went up and joined the singing.

a little history

Penguin Modern Classics were launched in 1961, and have been shaping the reading habits of generations ever since.

The list began with distinctive grey spines and evocative pictorial covers – a look that, after various incarnations, continues to influence their current design – and with books that are still considered landmark classics today.

Penguin Modern Classics have caused scandal and political change, inspired great films and broken down barriers, whether social, sexual or the boundaries of language itself. They remain the most provocative, groundbreaking, exciting and revolutionary works of the last 100 years (or so).

In 2011, on the fiftieth anniversary of the Modern Classics, we're publishing fifty Mini Modern Classics: the very best short fiction by writers ranging from Beckett to Conrad, Nabokov to Saki, Updike to Wodehouse. Though they don't take long to read, they'll stay with you long after you turn the final page.

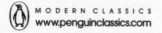

MODERN CLASSICS
www.penguinclassics.com